504

D0421871

ANTIQUE
FAIRY
TALES

ILLUSTRATOR'S NOTE

Myths and fairy tales are an important part of every culture. Illustrating these beautifully written and sensitive stories from all over the world has given me a wonderful opportunity to portray hippogriffs, dragons, giants, fairies, elves and other fanciful creatures. I felt young again as I went into their magic lands and became their friend. I hope my paintings will open windows into these worlds for others.

I've been painting since I was very young, and inherited my talent from my parents who are both artists in their own right. My mother excels in costume design and painting, and my father in sculpture, drawing, and model making. I've always liked collecting costumes, and many of the clothes the models wore, I made myself. Some of the most graceful models I find are, or were at one time, ballet dancers. The adult Flower Folk in "The Fairy Kingdom" are now, or were, dancers from the Pennsylvania and Milwaukee Ballet Company. This Ballet company also very graciously provided me with studio space for photographing, and costumes for "The Steadfast Tin Soldier".

Some tales that I have always wanted to illustrate have been included, such as "Thumbelina", "Cinderella", and "The Paradise of Children". Elves and fairies are some of my favorite beings, so I had a wonderful time painting "The Fairy Kingdom". With so many tiny, detailed creatures, I had to paint the original three times as large as it appears in the book. I also loved painting the very beautiful and very handsome, such as Cinderella, and the Prince in "The White Cat", as well as the macabre. The troubles coming out of Pandora's box were fascinating to draw, as well as the Giant with his unfortunate wife in "The Five Wise Words of the Guru". I also enjoyed painting lovely landscapes, and intricate interiors, such as the

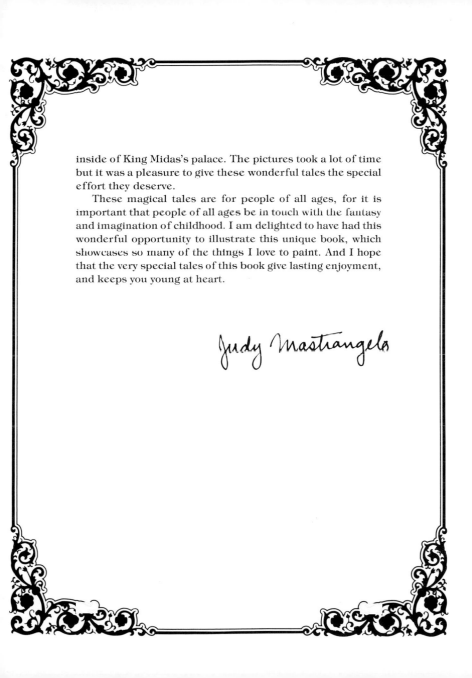

inside of King Midas's palace. The pictures took a lot of time but it was a pleasure to give these wonderful tales the special effort they deserve.

These magical tales are for people of all ages, for it is important that people of all ages be in touch with the fantasy and imagination of childhood. I am delighted to have had this wonderful opportunity to illustrate this unique book, which showcases so many of the things I love to paint. And I hope that the very special tales of this book give lasting enjoyment, and keeps you young at heart.

Judy Mastrangelo

ANTIQUE FAIRY TALES

Illustrated By
JUDY MASTRANGELO

The Unicorn Publishing House
New Jersey

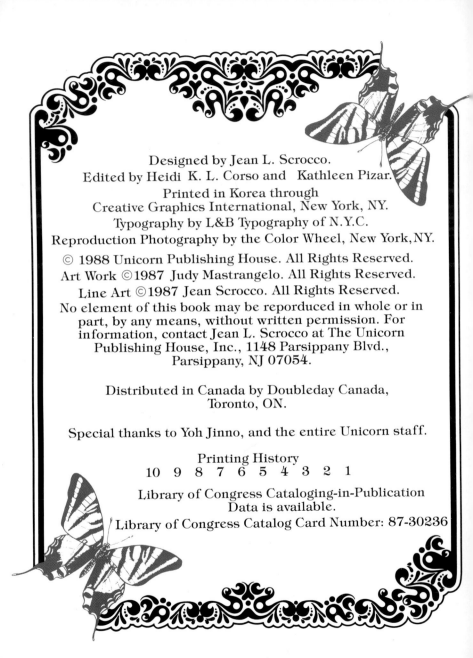

Designed by Jean L. Scrocco.
Edited by Heidi K. L. Corso and Kathleen Pizar.
Printed in Korea through
Creative Graphics International, New York, NY.
Typography by L&B Typography of N.Y.C.
Reproduction Photography by the Color Wheel, New York, NY.

© 1988 Unicorn Publishing House. All Rights Reserved.
Art Work ©1987 Judy Mastrangelo. All Rights Reserved.
Line Art ©1987 Jean Scrocco. All Rights Reserved.
No element of this book may be reporduced in whole or in
part, by any means, without written permission. For
information, contact Jean L. Scrocco at The Unicorn
Publishing House, Inc., 1148 Parsippany Blvd.,
Parsippany, NJ 07054.

Distributed in Canada by Doubleday Canada,
Toronto, ON.

Special thanks to Yoh Jinno, and the entire Unicorn staff.

Printing History
10   9   8   7   6   5   4   3   2   1

Library of Congress Cataloging-in-Publication
Data is available.
Library of Congress Catalog Card Number: 87-30236

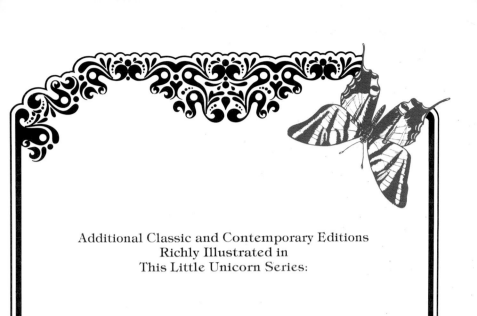

Additional Classic and Contemporary Editions
Richly Illustrated in
This Little Unicorn Series:

PINOCCHIO

THE WIZARD OF OZ

HEIDI

PETER PAN

CAST OF CHARACTERS

Elizabeth Leube • The Little Mermaid
Audrey G. Bookspan • The Sea Witch
Mary Ivy Bayard • The Prince's Bride
Jason Lubar • Mermaid's Prince; Fatima's Brother; Egyptian Prince
Francis X. McIlhenny • The Selfish Giant
Timothy Cunningham • The Boy in the Giant's Garden
Caryn Block • Wizard's Wife; Hands
Jack Kessler • Wizard
Sarah Armour • Swan Fairy's Daughter
Judy Mastrangelo • Swan Fairy
Marcy Nguyen • Li-Ho
Tai Thai • Wang
Rose Dyer • Pandora
Timothy Tracy • Epimetheus
Kathy L. Arena • Hope; Fairy Queen
Edward Meyers • Imps; Mercury; Flower Folk
Matthew Stokes • The Angel
Michael G. Mastrangelo • Angel Boy
Willie Adler • Blue Beard
Kimberly McCartney • Fatima
Gary Gresh • Fatima's Brother
John D. Haasz • The Happy Prince; White Cat's Prince
Joel Sokoloff • Fisherman; Indian Giant
J. Frederic Trenary • The Tin Soldier; The Flower Prince
Lauren Wright • The Ballerina
Trevor Shadow • Imp
Fredi Sokoloff • Fisherman's Wife
Danielle Capriotti • Cinderella
Stephanie Wolf Spassoff • The Fairy Godmother
Michael B. Mastrangelo • King Midas
Regina Szczesniak • Marygold
Matthew Blain • Jack
Mark Fitch • Giant
Brendan Dougherty • Tippitin
Melissa Johnsson Elstien • Thumbelina
Sari Braff • Flower Folk
Lisa Collins • Flower Folk
Reiko Kimura • Flower Folk
Kurt Kramer • Flower Folk
Veronica Lynn • Flower Folk
Albert Volk • Flower Folk
Walter Wood IV • Flower Folk

LIST OF ILLUSTRATIONS

THE LITTLE MERMAID

Far out in the deep blue ocean, in the clear water above the white bottom sand, strange trees move with the current and fish glide along. At the deepest spot, a palace stands with coral walls inset with amber windows. In it lives the widowed sea-king, his mother and six lovely sea-princesses.

The youngest princess was the most beautiful, with blue eyes and clear skin down to her silvery fishtail. The young mermaid tended a sea-garden of red-rose flowers the color of the sun, and in it stood a white marble statue of a handsome boy, which had sunk from some wreck long ago.

One afternoon while the grandmother was telling stories, she said to the princesses, "When you are fifteen years old, you will be allowed to rise to the surface of the sea, sit on the rocks and see the big ships, forests and towns." The following year, the eldest sister was fifteen and, as promised, she rose to the surface of the ocean. On her return, she told of lying on a sandbank in the moonlight. She heard the bustle of carriages and listened to music.

Next, the second sister went up: she described a golden sunset and a flock of wild swans, flying like a long white veil. Then the third princess swam boldly up a broad river and saw children playing. She wanted to join their play, but they ran away terrified and a small black dog barked at her.

The not-so-daring fourth sister stayed in the open sea with playful dolphins. The fifth sister's birthday was in winter; she saw a green sea with icebergs that looked like huge pearls.

At last, the youngest was fifteen and lifted her head out of the water. She saw a gaily-lit party boat nearby with a handsome prince dancing on the deck. Suddenly, a storm arose that tossed the ship violently until it sank. The mermaid rescued the unconscious prince from among the planks and swam with him to a warm beach. She kissed him, then hid behind the rocks and waited. Soon a group of girls from a convent school ran down the sand and a pretty girl with along dark lashes ran to help the prince. The lovely mermaid returned to her sisters.

Now each day, she went to watch humans and grew to love them. One day she happened upon the marble palace where the prince lived, and thereafter, she went in the evening to see him standing on the terrace in the moonlight.

Finally, the princess asked her grandmother if humans died other than by drowning. She said humans did die other ways and their life was not three hundred years like that of sea-folk, but also that humans had something called an immortal soul.

The mermaid decided to seek the advice of the sea witch that lived near the roaring whirlpools. The path to the witch was lined with sea animals with slimy fingers like wriggling worms, that grasped and clutched as she went by. She was afraid but she kept going. The princess passed snakes and the bleached bones of dead sailors. "I know what you want," said the witch, "it is silly, but you want legs so that the prince will fall in love with you, and you may win him and an immortal soul. To that end, I will make you a magical drink."

The Witch's Grotto

"It'll hurt to walk, like a sharp sword had split you," the witch said, "but you will appear a graceful child." The mermaid, trembling, took the drink and prepared to leave. "Remember," called the witch, "you can never be a mermaid again and if the prince marries another, the next morning your heart will break and you will be foam upon the water." In payment, the witch demanded the mermaid's beautiful voice.

The little mermaid swam to the prince's palace, drank the burning draft on the marble steps and fainted. When she awoke to the prince's gaze, her fishtail was gone. She became the prince's constant, though silent, companion and he grew very fond of her.

Although the prince knew that she was devoted to him, he told her that he was already betrothed to a beautiful princess whom he had never met.

One day, his betrothed was brought to the palace. He looked at her lovely eyes and said, "You are she who saved me!" Soon they were wed. That same evening, the bride and bridegroom came on board the ship, cannons roared and flags waved. In the middle of the ship stood a royal tent of purple and gold, with a couch for the couple to rest on through the night. The mermaid's sisters rose from the waves and tried to convince her to save her own life by killing the bride. Instead, the mermaid kissed the sleeping prince and leapt into the sea.

Transparent beings surrounded her. She was one of them, rising slowly out of the foam, all with melodious voices. They told her that by doing good deeds, she would earn an immortal soul.

The little mermaid lifted her eyes to the rising sun, and felt tears for the first time. She looked again at the ship, then rose to the clouds with the other children of the air.

Child of the Air

THE SELFISH GIANT

Every day, children played in the Selfish Giant's garden while he was away. There, flowers and peach trees blossomed pink in spring and bore fruit in autumn. "How happy we are here!" the children exclaimed. When the Giant returned, he cried in a gruff voice, "What are you doing?" and the children ran away. The Giant built a wall around his garden. Spring came, but not to the Giant's garden. With no children, the trees wouldn't bud. Snow and Frost stayed; North Wind and Hail visited often. "Spring is late," said the Giant wistfully.

One day, he noticed the children had crawled through a hole in the wall and were perched on blooming trees. Yet, one child was crying. He was too tiny to reach a branch. The Giant's heart softened and he lifted up the little boy. Suddenly, the tree burst into blossoms. Each day afterwards, all but the tiny boy returned. The Giant played happily with the children in his garden until he grew so old that he just watched, yet he never forgot the little boy.

Years later, the Giant saw the little boy again. It was winter, yet there was a tree in the farthest corner of the garden with white blossoms, golden branches and silver fruit. Beneath it stood the little boy with nail holes in his hands and feet. He said they were wounds of love. The child smiled at the old Giant, and said to him, "You let me play once in your garden, today you shall come with me to my garden, which is Paradise." When the children ran in that afternoon, they found the Giant lying dead under a tree that was covered with blossoms.

Spring, Winter and Fall

THE BLUE PARROT

In a part of Arabia which had palm trees and sweet-scented flowers, lived a young king, Lino. His people were happy and prosperous, but wished him to marry. An ambassador from a neighboring kingdom showed Lino a portrait of Princess Hermosa, the Swan fairy's daughter. Lino thought she was beautiful and it was arranged that they would marry. Unluckily for Lino, the magician Ismenor, a neighboring king, had a hideous daughter, Riquette. She loved Lino and begged her father to stop the wedding.

Ismenor summoned a humpbacked dwarf named Rabot and magically intercepted Lino and his party while they were on the road to the Swan fairy. With the use of spells, the magician exchanged the clothes of sleeping King Lino with the rags of Rabot. He made the dwarf assume Lino's shape in order to wed Princess Hermosa. Ismenor caught up King Lino in a cloud and returned to his palace.

Rabot actually believed he was king. When all awoke and the steward began, "May it please your majesty, I think . . ."

The false king, Rabot, interrupted: "Who told you to think? Get me some horse's flesh." The steward couldn't believe such rudeness.

Later, the Swan fairy and Hermosa met King Lino's party. Rabot ignored the princess. He had no memory of a portrait and said brusquely, "Let's have the wedding soon, meantime I need sleep."

As he snored upstairs, Hermosa wept. The Swan fairy consulted her mirror of truth, and beheld a sleeping dwarf and Lino in prison.

The Mirror's Vision

Immediately, the Swan fairy, as a swallow, flew with a letter to the prison in Ismenor's castle where Lino was being held. The letter asked Lino to pretend that he wanted to marry Riquette, and to claim that he needed Ismenor's magical stone to free himself from the spell of Hermosa. However, with the stone in the Swan fairy's possession, she could break Ismenor's power.

Lino did as the letter said. Unfortunately, the magician discovered that the Swan fairy was near. He turned the fairy and her subjects to stone. Hermosa was turned into a lovely tree in a forest. He transformed Lino into a blue parrot, saying, "A parrot you shall remain until Hermosa crushes your head."

The Blue Parrot flew about the world, until he was caught by the wife of a wizard. One day the Blue Parrot wrote a poem on the wizard's desk. The wizard realized that the bird was enchanted, and discovered the curse. He took the parrot to the forest and made three trees to fall together. Remembering the curse, the parrot flew under the loveliest tree. After the crash, Lino and Hermosa stood together.

Hermosa said that unless Ismenor was killed, the Swan fairy and her kingdom would be stone forever. Waiting until nightfall, the wizard went to Ismenor's palace and, changing himself into a bat, poured poisoned water over Ismenor's face and killed him.

Instantly, the Swan fairy became a woman again; Ismenor's spells were broken. When the Swan fairy returned to her capital, her courtiers, Hermosa and King Lino were waiting. Rabot became head of the stables.

After these terrible trials, they all felt sure that years of happiness lay ahead.

The Mystery of the Blue Parrot

THE HIPPOGRIFF AND THE DRAGON

In a shadowy cave, lived an old Dragon, who was the last of his tribe. Once he had killed and eaten people, but now he had just enough strength left to check his rabbit snares. Nearby dwelt a Hippogriff, the last of his race. Once, these two animals would have torn each other to pieces, but this pair were good friends. One day after a breakfast of cold crow wing, the Dragon suggested they seek employment in town. As they walked, they spied a maiden reading under a tree. "She wouldn't make a bad dinner," ventured the Hippogriff, timidly.

"Hush!" said the Dragon, and they approached her, expecting a blood-curdling shriek. However, this was an Advanced Young Woman who took them home, locked them in her study, and examined them scientifically. Each day, she came to feed them bowls of oatmeal for she had decided that they should become vegetarians. While they ate, she counted their vertebrae. She also decided that they should be donated to a museum for further study. She left the two of them in gloomy silence that evening, for they didn't want to be donated to a museum. It was then that they recalled the Fairy Vanishing Charm. As they chanted, they disappeared a piece at a time. As their backbones were vanishing, the Hippogriff gave a shout to think his vertebrae would never be counted again.

Soon they reappeared in the land of fairies. The next day, when she found that they were gone, The Advanced Young Woman shrugged her shoulders and decided, "They were just fabulous monsters I dreamed."

Old Friends

THE WILLOW TREE

Li-Ho was the beautiful daughter of a rich Chinese mandarin. If you could have seen her on a moonlit night, you would have thought her worthy to marry a prince. But Li-Ho loved Wang, a humble secretary.

Now her father had arranged for Li-Ho to wed old Ta-jin, who was very rich, when the peach tree bloomed in Spring. The willow tree was blooming now, for it was early in the year. Li-Ho was very sad, and prayed to the good Genii not to be parted from Wang. Wang was also sad, for Li-Ho's father had forbidden him to see her.

One night, Li-Ho saw a tiny boat floating on the pond. It held a poem from Wang. She wrote back that he should come for her before the peach tree blooms and they would elope.

The morning of Li-Ho's wedding to Ta-jin, she was dressed in blue silk with embroidered golden butterflies, because in China butterflies are looked upon as a symbol of married happiness. Ta-jin had sent Li-Ho a cask of brilliant jewels for a wedding gift, but she had no heart for them. An attendant entered the room and told Li-Ho that a servant wished to speak with her. "Let him come in," said Li-Ho, unhappily.

A young man entered wearing a long blue cotton robe and a broad straw hat which hid his face. As soon as they were alone, he took off his hat and made Li-Ho a low sweeping bow, and there was Wang himself! Li-Ho and Wang rushed out of the house, but Li-Ho's father spied the couple as they ran. With whip in hand, he rushed after them. The good Genii changed the lovers to two turtle-doves. The doves built a cozy nest in the garden where they could watch the willow and peach trees bloom and fade, without fear of being parted.

The Secret Romance

THE PARADISE OF CHILDREN

Long ago, when this world was in its tender infancy, everyone was a child, because there was no need for mothers and fathers. It was a pleasant life: no labor of any kind; nothing but pleasure all day. Those ugly little winged monsters, Troubles, were not yet on the earth.

Among the children was a boy named Epimetheus. So he wouldn't be lonely, a little girl, Pandora, was sent to live with him. The first thing that Pandora saw when she entered his cottage was a large carved box fastened by an intricately knotted cord. She asked him what was inside, but he said, "I don't know what is inside. A smiling man in a feathered cap and a staff with two carved serpents left it here."

"That is Quicksilver," said Pandora, "and it was he that brought me hither, as well as the box. Maybe it is intended for me."

"That may be so," said Epimetheus, "but it is not ours to open."

Pandora, however, gave Epimetheus no rest from her curiosity about the box. She beset him with questions about it, until he had grown extremely tired of the subject. One day, when Epimetheus was outside, Pandora was again examining the box. Inside she thought she heard a stifled murmur. "Let us out!" something whispered. She fingered the knot and the cord untwined itself as if by magic. She decided that she may as well look inside, for Epimetheus would assume she had. She lifted the lid just as Epimetheus came home. He didn't stop Pandora from what she was doing, for in truth, he was curious, too.

As the lid went up, a black swarm of winged creatures flew out. They were earthly Troubles, evil Passions, Cares, Sorrows and Diseases.

Pandora's Box

Instantly, Epimetheus cried out, "Oh, I am stung! Oh naughty Pandora! Why have you opened this wicked box?" Pandora let fall the lid and looked up. She heard a disagreeable buzzing, as if many huge insects were darting about. Suddenly, one settled on her forehead and would have stung her, if Epimetheus had not brushed it away.

The first thing that the two children did was to open the windows of their cottage in the hope of getting rid of them, and sure enough, the Troubles flew out and tormented all of the children of the world.

Pandora began crying bitterly, and Epimetheus sat sullenly in the corner. Suddenly, there was a gentle tap on the inside of the lid. "What can that be?" cried Pandora.

"Lift the lid and you shall see," said a sweet voice.

"Oh, no," said Pandora. "I have had enough of lifting the lid! You shall stay in the box, you naughty creature!" Pandora looked at Epimetheus, perhaps expecting that he would commend her for her wisdom, but the sullen boy only muttered that she was wise a little too late.

"I am not like those wicked creatures that hurt you," said the kindly little voice. "Only let me out and you shall see." And indeed, there was a kind of cheerful witchery in the voice that made it impossible to resist. With one consent, the children lifted the lid.

Out flew a smiling little person, with wings like a rainbow. She kissed Pandora and Epimetheus where the trouble had stung them, and both of their hurts disappeared right away. "I am Hope!" said the sunshiny figure as she flew around their room, spreading light and gladness. "I shall always stay with you to make amends for the wicked Troubles which were destined to be let out among you. Look for me when things seem their darkest, and you shall always find me."

Hope

THE ANGEL

Whenever a good child dies, an angel flies with the child to all the places which were dear. The child gathers flowers and plants them in Heaven, where each is given a voice with which to sing in the heavenly choir. That was what an Angel told a child whom it was carrying up to Heaven as they visited places where the child had played. They gathered both gorgeous flowers and common daisies. "Now we have flowers enough," said the child, and although the Angel nodded, they still did not fly up to Heaven.

It was night and everything was silent. In a narrow street, the Angel picked up a broken pot with a flower still clinging to the moldy earth. "I will tell you a story," said the Angel. "There was once a boy who could not walk. One day, his friend brought him some field flowers, among which was one with a root. The little boy placed it in a flower pot close to his bed, where he could look at it every day. To the sick boy, it became the loveliest garden — his only treasure on earth. He watered it and tended it until the very last. Towards it he turned when God called him to his heavenly rest. For a year he has been with God, and for a year the flower has stood in the window, unheeded and forgotten, till it has been cast in the street as useless."

"But how do you know all this?" asked the child.

"I know this because I was the suffering boy and I have not forgotten my flower." They arrived in Heaven and the child was given wings that he could fly with his friend, hand in hand. And God kissed the poor field flower and it was given a voice to sing His praises.

Heavenly Companions

BLUE BEARD

There was in former times, a rich gentleman with fine houses and grand carriages, and immense wealth. He was known as Blue Beard, for unfortunately, he had a blue beard which was very frightening.

There was a lady of rank who had two daughters. Blue Beard asked her to bestow one upon him for his wife, but neither daughter wanted to marry him. The truth was, besides their fright at his blue beard, they knew that he had married several wives and that nobody knew what had become of them. In order to gain favor, Blue Beard invited the girls and some of their friends to a grand party which was to last a week, at one of his villas. The youngest had such fun, that she consented to marry him.

About a month after the wedding, Blue Beard was called out of town. He gave his bride a key to every room in his house, but forbade her to enter one little closet. "Don't enter that room," he said, "or you will have a terrible punishment!"

But her curiosity was too great; as soon as her husband left, she unlocked the door. She saw a bloody floor and the heads of several dead women, Blue Beard's former wives. In shock, the woman dropped the key to the floor. The key was stained with blood.

When Blue Beard returned, he knew she had disobeyed. She begged for mercy. He said, "Madam, you must die this very minute," and left to fetch his sword. Luckily, her brothers arrived just as Blue Beard was about to kill her. They slew him, and his wife inherited all Blue Beard's immense wealth, and lived happily ever after.

The Brothers' Rescue

THE WHITE CAT

Once upon a time there was a king who had three sons so clever and brave that he feared they would want to reign over the kindgom before he died. Although he was growing old, the king wasn't prepared to give up the government of his kingdom, so he explained to his sons that his successor would have to earn the throne with deeds. The king said, "I promise that the one who brings me the most beautiful little dog within one year shall have the throne." The princes were all surprised by this contest, but as it gave the two younger ones a chance that they would not otherwise have of being king, and the eldest was too polite to object, they began their search for a dog.

The three princes separated and went on their way. The youngest son, who was handsome and courageous, came upon a porcelain castle one rainy night. He pulled at the bell, and the door opened. A number of hands, which floated in the air, replaced his muddy clothes with rich ones. Then he was led to a reclining couch, where an orchestra of cats was tuning up their instruments.

The door opened and in came a tiny figure covered by a long, black veil. The little figure came up to him and threw off her veil. It was the loveliest white cat, but she looked very sad. She said in a sweet little voice, "Welcome, King's son. The Queen of the Cats is glad to see you." She ordered a banquet to be served, and the musicians to play. The prince was quite taken aback, but gave himself over to enjoying the evening. During the banquet, the Prince noticed that the White Cat wore a bracelet with a portrait which looked like himself.

Queen of the Cats

The next day, they went hunting — the White Cat rode a monkey, while the Prince was mounted on a painted wooden horse, which pranced quite gaily. That evening there were games and music and merriment. The days passed until the year was nearly over. One day, the White Cat said to him, "It is time for you to return to your father, and bring that which you sought." Holding an acorn, the White Cat said, "Here is the prettiest dog in the world. Crack the shell carefully."

When the Prince opened the acorn, inside was the tiniest, prettiest dog in the world. But the king was not yet ready to give up his reign, so he asked his sons to find a length of muslin which could pass through the eye of a needle. The youngest brother went to the White Cat, and was given a walnut. Inside was a lovely length of muslin that passed through the eye of the finest needle.

Now the king set them to find the most beautiful princess in the world. Again the Prince went to the White Cat, but when it was time to go, the Cat said, "Cut off my head." The Prince begged her not to ask that, but the cat looked so sorrowful that he did as he was told. Suddenly in front of him stood the most beautiful girl he had ever seen. "You have released me from an enchantment," said the girl. "Long ago the fairies who brought me up, grew angry when I fell in love with a mortal prince. They turned me into a white cat, and said that I would remain that way until I met a prince who in every way resembled the first prince I fell in love with."

The Prince brought the Princess to his father, who found her the most beautiful Princess in the world. But as she had her own kingdom to rule, and enough kingdoms for the Prince's brothers, the king continued to rule his own country happily, until the end of his days.

The Royal Hunt

THE FIVE WISE WORDS OF THE GURU

Once there was a man named Ram Singh who determined to seek his fortune. When his wise guru learned of Ram Singh's plan, he said, "Remember these five counsels, and you shall do well. First — obey your master's orders; second — never speak unkindly; third — never lie; fourth — never try to be the equal of those above you; and fifth — listen to those who read from the holy books, so you may grow wise."

Ram Singh quickly obtained a position as servant to the rajah. One day, the rajah and his servants journeyed across a desert. When they stopped to rest, there was no water, but there was a well which was said to be haunted. The rajah ordered Ram Singh to go to the well for water. Obeying his master, Ram Singh went to the well and met a giant holding a skeleton. "What think you of my lovely wife?" said the giant. Remembering the guru's second warning, Ram Singh said, "Surely, you could find nowhere such another." The giant was pleased and gave Ram Singh water. As a reward, the rajah made Ram Singh his treasurer. Now the rajah's brother, the Prince, wanted to obtain the rajah's money, but Ram Singh was very honest. So he offered Ram Singh his daughter's hand in marriage. Remembering the guru's fourth counsel, Ram Singh respectfully declined the offer. The Prince was determined to kill Ram Singh. He sent Ram Singh to check on a tower being built, but Ram Singh stopped to listen to a holy man. The army was to kill anyone asking questions, so that when the Prince went to see what was keeping Ram Singh, the Prince's head was cut off by mistake. Ram Singh continued to serve the rajah faithfully for the rest of his life.

In the Depths of the Well

THE STEADFAST TIN SOLDIER

There were once five and twenty tin soldiers who lived in a box together. The twenty-fifth soldier only had one leg for there was not enough tin left to finish him. He stood very firmly though.

On the nursery table where they stood, there were many toys, but the prettiest was a cardboard castle with a little cardboard Dancer. She had on a dress of the finest muslin and a little blue sash with a glittering tinsel star on it, and she raised one leg so high behind her that the Tin Soldier thought that she had only one leg like himself.

"She would be just the wife for me," thought the Tin Soldier, "but she is highborn and lives in a castle, while I only live in a box, and that there are twenty-five of us to share. Nevertheless, I will try to make her acquaintance."

At night, the Tin Soldier stood staring at the little Dancer, for he had fallen deeply in love. Suddenly, Bang! opened the lid of another little box. Inside was an imp who said, "Soldier, keep your eyes to yourself!" But the Soldier paid no attention. "Well, you just wait till tomorrow," said the imp.

The next morning, the Tin Soldier was placed on a window ledge. Whether it was a draught or the imp I do not know, but the Soldier fell headlong from the second story into the street. The servant and the little boy went down at once to look for him, and had the Soldier called out, they would have found him, no doubt. But he did not consider it soldier-like to shout while in uniform. Two street urchins found him, and they made a boat out of newspaper and sailed the Soldier through the gutter.

Steadfast Love

Suddenly, the boat drifted under a bridge, and a large rat appeared. "Have you got a pass?" he squeaked. The Tin Soldier did not reply, and his boat shot along. The rat shrieked out, "Stop him! Stop him! He hasn't got a pass! He has not paid his toll!"

Being only a paper boat, it soon filled with water and sank. The Tin Soldier thought of the pretty little Dancer, whom he should never see again. At that moment, a large fish swallowed the Soldier. Oh, how dark it was in there! And so little room!

The fish began to jump about in the most violent manner, but all of a sudden it became very quiet. The fish was caught and sold. A cook was cutting it up with a big knife when she found the Tin Soldier. She placed him on a table and — wonder of wonders! — he found himself on the same nursery table, with the pretty little Dancer waiting for him. He looked at her and she at him, but neither said anything.

Suddenly, a little boy threw the Soldier right into the fire. It was, no doubt, the imp's doing again.

The Soldier stood in the full glare and felt a heat quite dreadful; but whether it was the fire or love, he knew not. He had quite lost his colors, but nobody could tell whether on the journey or through grief. He looked at the little maiden and she looked at him; he felt he was melting, but he still stood firm. Just then a door opened and the draft caught the cardboard Dancer who flew right into the fire where the Tin Soldier stood, blazed up and disappeared.

When the servant removed the ashes from the fire in the morning, she found the Soldier in the form of a little tin heart, and of the Dancer, only the tinsel star remained, and that was burned black as coal.

Escape From the Rats

THE FISHERMAN AND HIS WIFE

A fisherman once lived with his wife in a tiny hut. One day, when he was fishing, he pulled up his line and had caught a large flounder.

"Let me go," said the fish. "I am not a real fish, but a prince."

The man had pity on the fish and released it. That night, he told his wife about the fish. His wife said, "If the fish was magic, you could have wished for a better hut than this one. Call him. Maybe he will answer."

So the fisherman went back to the shore and said, "Flounder, flounder in the sea; Come, I have a wish for thee."

The fish came to the surface and asked, "What do you want?"

The fisherman replied, "My wife says that I should have wished for a better house than the one that we have."

"Go home," said the fish. "She is in it already."

The fisherman went home and found his wife in a pretty cottage. But the wife said, "This is too small. Ask the flounder for a castle."

The fisherman went unwillingly to the sea and asked the flounder. "Go home," said the flounder. "She is in it already."

Home again, the fisherman saw his wife seated in a great castle. "Tell the flounder that I want to be Pope." she said. Her husband reluctantly, went to the shore and asked the Fish to make her Pope.

"Go home," said the Fish. "She is Pope already." The fisherman went home and found his wife with thousands of candles lit around her while kings knelt before her and kissed her slippers.

The Blaze of Candles

Her husband stood for a time watching her and said, "Well, wife, now you are Pope."

"Yes," she said, "I am."

"You cannot be higher than a Pope, so now, I suppose you are content?"

"I am not quite sure," she said. But when evening came and they retired to rest, she could not sleep for thinking of what she should next wish for. Her husband slept soundly, for he had tired himself out the day before; but she rose even before the day broke, and stood at the window to watch the sun rise.

It was a beautiful sight, and as she watched it, she exclaimed, "Oh! If only I had the power to make the sun rise! Husband, wake up!" she said, jabbing him in the ribs. "Go and tell your fish that I wish to be equal to the Creator, and make the sun rise."

The husband was so frightened at this that he tumbled out of bed and fell on his knees before her and begged her not to make this demand, but she flew into a rage and drove him from the house. The poor fisherman went down to the shore in terror, for a dreadful storm had risen and he could scarcely stand on his feet. Ships were wrecked, boats tossed to and fro, and rocks rolled into the sea.

In his terror and confusion he heard a voice from amid the storm: "Your wife wishes to be equal to the Creator. Go home, man, and find her again in the poor hut by the sea!"

He went home to find the glories and the riches and the palaces had vanished, and his wife sitting in their old hut, an example of the consequences of impious ambition.

A Well-Deserved End

CINDERELLA

Long ago there was a gentle girl named Cinderella, who had lost her beloved mother. Her father remarried a haughty widow with two haughty daughters. The stepsisters were jealous of Cinderella's beauty and kindness. They dressed her in rags and made her work very hard.

Now the King's son was giving a grand ball. The stepsisters were invited, but Cinderella was not allowed to go. When the night of the ball came, Cinderella stood in the garden and watched her sisters' coach drive away. As she cried, her fairy godmother appeared and said with a smile, "Do not cry, for you shall go to the ball, lovely child." The godmother waved her wand over a pumpkin and, instantly, it became a fine coach. Then she waved her wand over Cinderella's rags and they became a beautiful dress of gold and silver; upon her feet were delicate glass slippers. "My magic ends at midnight," her godmother warned, "so you must leave the ball before the stroke of twelve."

Cinderella had a lovely time dancing with the handsome Prince. As she left, she lost one of her glass slippers, and the Prince picked it up. He said that he would marry whoever's foot would fit in the tiny slipper, for he had fallen in love with Cinderella. All of the ladies tried on the little slipper, but found it too small. When the Prince's messenger came to Cinderella's home, she tried on the slipper and of course, it fit perfectly. The Prince recognized Cinderella as the beautiful lady at the ball, and so he married her and they lived happily ever after.

The Fairy Godmother's Gift

THE GOLDEN-HEADED FISH

Once in Egypt lived a king who had lost his sight from a bad illness. Therefore, great was the rejoicing when a visiting doctor said that he could cure the King. "Somewhere in the sea," he said, "is a Golden-Headed Fish. I can make an ointment from its blood that will cure the King. For one hundred days I will wait here, but if the Fish is not caught by that time, I must return to my own country."

After one hundred days of searching, the Prince caught the Fish. As it was too late to cure his father, he had pity on the Fish and let it go. The King condemned the Prince to death when he heard of his mercy, but the Prince escaped and sailed away. He arrived on a beautiful island, bought a fine house, and hired an Arab as a servant.

Now the Prince fell in love with a beautiful Princess and her father agreed to their marriage. He warned the Prince that the Princess had been married many times, but each time her husband had died within twelve hours. The Prince was so in love that he married her anyway.

On the wedding night, a poisonous snake leapt from the mouth of the bride as they were having dinner. The faithful Arab caught and killed the snake, and the curse that was on the bride was removed.

A few days later, the servant asked permission to leave the service of the Prince. The Prince was sad, but gave him permission, gratefully, saying, "Without you, I should have long ago been dead."

"And without you, I should have long ago been dead," said the faithful Arab. "I am the Golden-Headed Fish."

Magic From the Sea

THE GOLDEN TOUCH

Once there was a king named Midas, who had a daughter named Marygold. Now King Midas loved gold dearly and, at length (as people always grow more and more foolish unless they take care to grow wiser and wiser), he spent all of his time counting it. One day Midas was in his vault, when he looked up and saw the figure of a young man with a gleaming smile and a cheerful face.

As Midas knew that he had carefully locked himself inside his vault, he concluded that his visitor was more than mortal. The stranger gazed about the room, and said, "You are a wealthy man, friend Midas."

"I have done pretty well," said Midas slowly.

"Then you are not content?" asked the stranger. "Tell me, what would make you happy?"

Midas paused. He had an idea that this stranger had both the power and intention to grant his wish, so he said, "I wish that everything I touched would be turned to gold."

"The Golden Touch!" exclaimed the stranger with a broad smile. "Be it as you wish then. Tomorrow at sunrise you will find yourself gifted with the Golden Touch." The stranger then began to glow, and Midas closed his eyes. When he opened them, he was alone again.

When Midas awoke the next day, he was delighted to find that his bedclothes had become pure gold. He leapt out of bed and put his hands on everything he could find. But when he put on his spectacles, he was dismayed; the glass had turned to gold, making them useless.

The Gift of the God

Still, King Midas was so exalted by his good fortune, that the palace didn't seem big enough to hold him. He went out to his garden which was filled with roses, and painstakingly turned each into gold. Happily, he went in to breakfast. A little later, Marygold came in crying bitterly. She had run to gather roses for her father and found they no longer smelled sweetly. Too ashamed to confess, Midas began eating. He bit into a potato, and found his mouth full of hot metal which burnt his tongue so that he roared.

Marygold ran to her father to comfort him. But alas! As soon as he touched her, little Marygold became a golden statue!

Midas wrung his hands, realizing what a curse his love of gold had put on him. Suddenly, the stranger appeared in front of him. "Well, friend Midas, have you made a discovery since yesterday?"

"Gold is not everything," said Midas, "and I have lost all that my heart ever really cared for."

"You are wiser than you were," said the stranger. "If you wish to rid yourself of the Golden Touch, plunge into the river. Take a vase of water and sprinkle it over anything you wish changed back." Midas snatched up a vase and leapt into the river. He ran back to his palace and sprinkled great handfuls of water on little Marygold. No sooner did it fall on her than you would have laughed to see the rosy color come back to her cheeks. Then he took her by the hand and sprinkled water over the roses. He was overjoyed to see them bloom as they did before.

When Midas had grown old, he was fond of telling this marvelous story to Marygold's children. He would stroke their glossy gold ringlets and say, "and to tell you the truth, precious children, since that morning I have hated the sight of any other gold save this."

The Curse of the Golden Touch

JACK AND THE BEANSTALK

Once there was a poor widow with a son named Jack. As they were dreadfully poor, the widow decided to sell her cow, and she sent Jack to the market with the beast. On his way, Jack met a butcher who offered to trade him some magic beans for his cow. Jack agreed, but when he told his mother, she was very vexed and shed many tears, scolding Jack for his folly. She angrily flung the beans out the window.

In the morning, Jack was astonished to see a huge beanstalk outside. He climbed it and found himself in a beautiful country. Ahead of him was a fine castle.

As he walked forward, he met a woman in a red cap. "Jack," she said, "this castle once belonged to your father, who was a knight. Inside lives an evil Giant who killed your father and stole his property. Your mother has kept the guise of a peasant woman, to remain in safety, for the Giant has vowed to kill her also." The woman nodded at him and disappeared, and Jack realized that she was a fairy.

He stole into the castle and hid in the wardrobe until the Giant came home. The Giant thundered in and sat down to a huge meal. Then he pulled out some bags of gold and counted his money. Jack waited until the Giant fell asleep and stole softly to the bags of gold, which were his very own as they had belonged to his father. He picked them up and ran off. With great difficulty he descended the beanstalk and laid the gold down in front of his mother.

Jack Steals the Giant's Plunder

Jack's mother was very glad to get the money, but she did not like him to run any risk for her. After a time, Jack decided to return to the Giant's castle. He climbed the beanstalk once more, and hid in the wardrobe. The Giant came to supper, and Jack watched him through the keyhole. When the Giant had eaten another huge meal, he reached for a beautiful fairy harp, sparkling with diamonds, rubies, and golden strings.

"Play," the Giant commanded, and at once a beautiful lullaby flowed from the harp. The Giant closed his eyes at the sweet notes and drifted off to sleep.

Jack sprang from the closet and seized the harp, but as he jumped over the threshold of the castle, the harp called, "Master! Master!"

The Giant woke up. With a tremendous roar he leapt from his chair and in two strides had reached the door.

Jack was very nimble. He fled like lightning with the fairy harp, talking to it as he went and telling it that he was the son of its old master. Jack hastened down the beanstalk, but just as he reached his garden, he beheld the Giant descending after him. "Mother! Mother!" he cried, "Make haste and give me the axe!" His mother ran to him with an axe and Jack cut down the beanstalk. He darted away and the Giant fell with a terrible crash and died.

Before Jack and his mother had recovered from their alarm, the old woman with the red cap appeared. "Jack," she said, "You have acted like a brave knight's son and deserve to have your inheritance restored to you. By showing an inquiring mind, great courage and enterprise, you shall live happily ever after." And so he did.

Jack Escapes From the Giant

THE HAPPY PRINCE

High above the city on a tall column stood the statue of the Happy Prince. He was gilded all over with thin leaves of fine gold, had two bright sapphires for eyes, and a large red ruby glowed on his sword hilt. He was very much admired by the townspeople.

A little Swallow, who was flying to the warm lands of Egypt to spend the winter, saw the statue and decided to sleep there and continue traveling in the morning. He settled down between the Prince's feet. "I have a golden bedroom," he said softly. Then he felt a large drop of water fall on him. He looked up and saw tears running down the face of the Prince. He was so beautiful in the moonlight that the bird pitied him. "Why are you weeping?" asked the Swallow.

"When I was alive and had a human heart," said the Prince, "I lived in a great palace where sorrow was not allowed to enter. But when I died, they put me up here where I can see the misery of my people, and I cannot help but weep. Far away," continued the statue, "there is a woman with a sick child who is too poor to cure him. Little Swallow, will you take her the ruby from my sword? My feet are fastened to this pedestal and I cannot move."

The Happy Prince looked so sad that the Swallow said, "It is very cold here, but I will stay for one night and be your messenger."

The next morning, the Swallow pulled out the ruby and brought it to the poor woman. He felt much warmer now, although the weather was cold, because of his good action.

The Princely Statue

The Swallow slept at the feet of the Prince again that night. In the morning he was to fly to Egypt, but the Prince said, "Swallow, little Swallow, I see a young author who is starving. Pluck a sapphire from my eye, and bring it to him." The Swallow obeyed, and slept again that night at the feet of the Happy Prince. The next day the Prince said, "I see a young match girl who has lost the matches that she was to sell. Her father will beat her if she does not bring home some money. Bring the other sapphire from my other eye to her."

The Swallow did so, then returned to the Prince. "Now you are blind," he said, "so I shall stay with you always."

The next day the Prince said, "Take off the gold I am covered in, and give it to the poor." The Swallow did as the Prince wished. The Happy Prince now looked dull and gray, but he was filled with joy, for the townspeople were happy.

The snow came, but the poor Swallow would not leave his friend the Prince. He grew colder and colder. At last he knew he was going to die. He flew up to the Prince's shoulder and kissed him. "Goodbye, dear Prince," he murmured, and fell dead at the Prince's feet. At that moment, the Prince's leaden heart broke in two.

The townspeople noticed how shabby the Happy Prince looked, so they took down the statue to melt it. The heart would not melt so they took it and threw it on a dust heap where they had thrown the Swallow.

"Bring me the two most precious things in the city," said God to an Angel. The Angel brought up to heaven the leaden heart and the dead Swallow, and in the Garden of Paradise the Swallow and the Happy Prince sang the praises of God forever.

The Parting of Friends

THE ONE-FOOTED FAIRY

There once was a fairy who sat down while the others were dancing. His name was Tippitin, and he was a very happy fairy, usually, but one night he was sad and wouldn't dance.

It happened the night that the fairies were busy preparing for the return of the Fairy Queen who had been visiting the North. The night before, they had discovered that the Queen's favorite throne was unsteady. Perhaps a rabbit or mortal may have hit it by accident and it had wiggled. But that night when the fairies inspected it, the throne didn't wiggle at all. They began practicing a welcoming dance, when they noticed a gap in the fairy ring. "Tippitin, come dance," they called.

"I don't want to dance," said Tippitin gruffly, and he remained sitting on a pebble with a leaf tucked over his knees.

At twelve o'clock, the grasshoppers and the crickets brought out their musical instruments and began to play. The Queen of the Fairies appeared, driving a splendid ice chariot drawn by the Northern Lights. It was the most beautiful carved ice you ever saw, and the canopy over it was the loveliest spun frost. The fairies began their welcoming dance, but Tippitin still sat in a dark corner, wrapped in a shadow.

"It is a nice dance," said the Queen, "but something is missing." She sat down on her throne. "I am not quite sure what it is, but it is something very fast and sure, that always comes down in the right place. Let me see it again."

Drawn by the Northern Lights

So the fairies began to dance all the more gaily, for they were afraid that the Queen would notice that Tippitin was not dancing, and that she would be angry. Presently, the Queen cried out, "Stop! Stop!" The dance stopped. "I should like to be told," she said, rather grandly, "what is the matter with this throne."

"Your majesty," cried the fairies, "it is your very own favorite throne."

"So I thought," said the Queen, "but there is something under it that keeps moving."

Suddenly, from under the throne danced the tiniest foot you ever saw. It danced straight up to Tippitin who still sat wrapped in his shadow. When Tippitin saw it, he stood up and threw off the shadow, and the fairies saw that he had only one foot. The little foot hopped up to his ankle. Tippitin bent down and screwed it on and made a beautiful low bow to the Queen. "Your majesty," he said, "The other day I found a little hollow under your throne that made it jiggle. I couldn't find anything that filled up the hollow exactly, except my foot, so I took it off and filled the hollow with it."

The Queen was very much affected, and said, "Henceforth, Tippitin is to be the keeper of my throne. And if he finds cause to think it needs repair, he may call upon all of the clever workmen of my kingdom to set it right again. But his own feet are needed for my service in dancing, so now fairies, to the dance!"

The fairies danced again, this time with no gap in their ring. When it was over, the Queen clapped her hands and said, "Now I see what was missing from the dance! It was Tippitin! And now it is the most perfectly lovely dance that ever was!"

The Gallant Bow

THUMBELINA

Once there was a women who went to an old witch and said, "I would very much like to have a small child; can you tell me where I can get one?"

The old witch gave her a seed and said, "Plant this seed." The woman thanked the Witch. She planted the seed and a beautiful flower bud grew. The woman kissed the bud and it opened. In the center of the flower sat a tiny maiden, delicately and gracefully formed. She was scarcely a thumb's length high, so she was called Thumbelina.

A neat, polished walnut shell served as a bed for Thumbelina. Blue violet leaves were her mattress and a rose petal was her blanket. During the daytime she played about on the table in a dish of water which the woman had put out for her. On this water there was a large tulip leaf and on this she could sit and row from one side of the dish to the other, using two white horse hairs for oars. She was a charming sight to see.

One night, an old toad crept through the window. Seeing Thumbelina asleep, the toad said, "She would be a pretty wife for my son." She picked up the walnut and brought it outside into a wide brook, where she placed the cradle on a lily pad.

The old toad brought her son to see Thumbelina. "Croak, croak, crek-keh-keh!" was all he could say when he saw the pretty girl. Thumbelina awoke, and the old toad said, "Here is my son, who you will marry, and forever live with us in the marsh." Thumbelina began to cry.

An Unwelcome Bridegroom

Suddenly, a cockchafer spied Thumbelina on the lily pad and he flew down and grasped her firmly around the waist. Then he flew her up to a tree, and told her that she was quite pretty, even if she was not a cockchafer. The other cockchafers did not agree, and chased Thumbelina away, because she had only two legs and no feelers.

A field mouse felt sorry for poor Thumbelina and invited her into her home. All winter long Thumbelina lived with the field mouse and was visited by the mouse's friend, a black mole. The mole grew so fond of Thumbelina that he dug a tunnel from his house to the mouse's home so that they could visit each other.

Now in this tunnel lay a swallow, which looked as though it had died of the cold. Thumbelina was grieved, and covered the swallow with warm hay that he might lie in peace. But the bird was not dead, he was only numb, and being warm again brought him back to life. Thumbelina nursed him tenderly until Spring came.

Now the mole asked the field mouse for permission to marry Thumbelina. The field mouse readily said yes, although Thumbelina did not wish to marry the mole.

So the swallow helped Thumbelina escape, and carried her far away, to a land of flowers and placed her down on the prettiest flower. Inside the flower was the king of the flower people. When he spied Thumbelina, he took the crown from his head and placed it on hers, asking her to be his wife. Thumbelina agreed, and from every flower came little people with gifts. The gift she liked best was a pair of beautiful wings from a large white fly; these were fastened onto her back, so that she could fly from flower to flower. There was much rejoicing at the wedding, and they all lived happily ever after.

The Fairy Kingdom

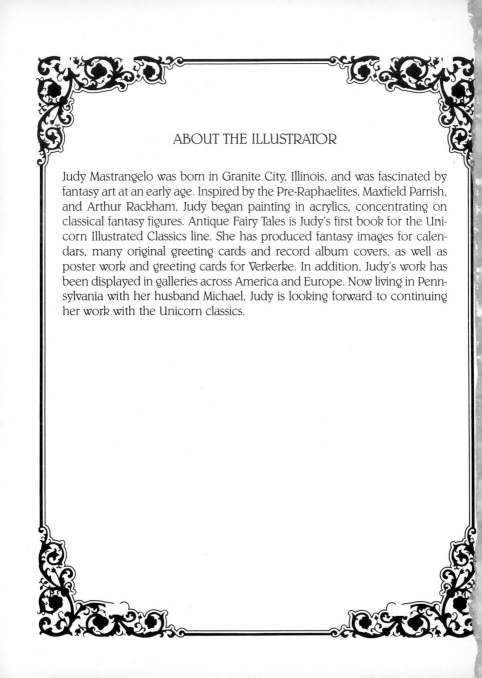

ABOUT THE ILLUSTRATOR

Judy Mastrangelo was born in Granite City, Illinois, and was fascinated by fantasy art at an early age. Inspired by the Pre-Raphaelites, Maxfield Parrish, and Arthur Rackham, Judy began painting in acrylics, concentrating on classical fantasy figures. Antique Fairy Tales is Judy's first book for the Unicorn Illustrated Classics line. She has produced fantasy images for calendars, many original greeting cards and record album covers, as well as poster work and greeting cards for Verkerke. In addition, Judy's work has been displayed in galleries across America and Europe. Now living in Pennsylvania with her husband Michael, Judy is looking forward to continuing her work with the Unicorn classics.